The Warmest Place on Ice

This book belongs to

_____

Mrs. Claus Explains It All

(At Last) Answers to the Questions Real Kids Ask!

by Elsbeth Claus • Illustrated by David Wenzel

Hello friends, Mrs. Claus here. It's nearly Thanksgiving and things are really heating up at the North Pole, which we like to call the warmest place on ice.

One of my favorite responsibilities as Santa's second-in-command is sorting and helping answer your letters to Santa. Each year we receive enormous piles of letters and email, and it occurred to me that perhaps I should address the most frequently asked questions from all you curious children.

So, I'm taking time out from my busy schedule to share with you some interesting details about life here at the North Pole, some of which have never been revealed before.

If you're ready, let's begin!

Dear Mrs. Claus,
Why can't you see
Santa's village at the North Pole?
How does it stay hidden?

There is a dense fog that floats like a dome over the village that is created by special cloud-making machines, so you can't see the village from the ground or the air. Some of the buildings, especially the newer workshops and warehouses, are underground. You'd be amazed at how big the entire complex is!

Dear Mrs. Claus, What is your house like?

The dining hall is big enough for every citizen of Santa's village to dine at once. It's huge!

To make life easier, we have built covered passageways that lead from our kitchen to our greenhouses and livestock barns.

The wardrobe department is where all our clothing is made, including the Elves' work uniforms and even dolls' outfits.

Upstairs are Santa's and my private quarters. We spend what little free time we have relaxing there—reading, chatting, or even napping!

Besides what I've already described, there is also our library, gymnasium, laundry, workshops, and warehouses, sleigh garage, reindeer stables, assembly hall, and of course, Elf Village.

Dear Mrs Claus,
How old are you
and Santa?

We are very old to be sure. You can't really count our age in typical years, as time is different here at the North Pole. I will say though, that we're older than dragons and younger than dinosaurs.

Dear Mrs Claus,
Do you have
any children?

Santa and I consider all the children in the world to be our "kids."

Dear Mrs. Claus,
Why do you still look
so young?

What a sweet thing to say! As I told you, here at the top of the world, time runs a bit differently. Everyone who lives here is quite old, even the reindeer, and none of us look our real age. The other factor is that we all live together quite happily, working toward a common goal. Love can truly keep you young at heart and the rest of you is bound to follow.

Dear Mrs. Claus,
How do you get your food up there?

Believe it or not, we have almost everything we need right here. We grow most of our food in giant greenhouses. We also have a large cozy barn where we keep our animals, including our special flock of sheep and goats, whose coats grow ten times faster than regular ones. The things we don't have are shipped to a secret location far outside the North Pole and are retrieved by Driver Elves and our reindeer-in-training, hauling a cargo sleigh.

Dear Mrs Claus,
What is Santa's favorite cookie?

Well, I've yet to come across a kind of cookie he doesn't like, but among his all-time favorites are chocolate chip (with or without nuts), gingersnaps, peanut butter, and oatmeal. (He loves when I put butter-scotch chips in his oatmeal cookies.)

Dear Mrs. Claus,
What does Santa like to eat?

Santa's favorite meal is macaroni-n-cheese. He is especially crazy for strawberries, which we grow year round so he can have strawberries and cream whenever he pleases. He doesn't like vegetables too much, but I do insist he have at least one with every meal. When it comes to veggies, he prefers carrots, string beans, and, believe it or not, broccoli!

Dear Mrs. Claus,
I'm worried that Santa is too fat. Does he ever exercise?

Santa is certainly plump, there's no denying that. He's a big fan of my home cooking and our Chef and Baker Elves are among the best, but he's surprisingly fit and limber—he has to be to accomplish all his deliveries on Christmas Eve. It may surprise you to learn that everyone, Santa and myself included, do at least one hour of exercise every day in our state-of-the-art underground gymnasium. We do everything from jumping jacks, trampoline, rope climbing, to dance aerobics!

Dear Mrs. Claus,
How did Santa get his sui
Has he always dressed
this way?

Not always. In the early days, Santa wore a hooded robe made of dark green velvet.

But over time, Santa realized that trousers and a jacket that didn't hang on the ground or get caught on loose roof shingles were more practical for shimmying in and out of chimneys.

The red suit came about really by accident when the head seamstress in the wardrobe department ran out of the green velvet. She used some crimson velvet she had on hand for stockings and such.

Well, the effect was so spectacular we all agreed that Santa should wear red from then on!

Dear Mrs Claus,
What are Santa's
Workshops like?

The original workshops are pretty basic: one large room with shelves on the walls to hold parts and tools and long work benches lined with stools. Early on, simple conveyor belts were used to send finished toys to the warehouses to be wrapped, tagged, and stored. Today this simple setup has become a giant complex of workshops, warehouses, and gift-wrap stations. Newer workshops have been built so there is only one story above ground, with two or more below.

The Underground Annex

Our modern workshops are housed in what we call the Underground Annex. These workshops are equipped with an elaborate system of pulleys, robotic arms, and special conveyors that climb and turn like a roller-coaster.

We are always eager to try new technologies and sometimes we're the first to test them out for the rest of the world.

To keep everyone cheerful, we hire elves with pleasant voices to read aloud to the others. As the holidays near and excitement builds, our Reader Elves are replaced by Music Elves who lead our hard-working staff in sing-a-longs.

Dear Mrs. Claus,
How does Santa know where I live? How does he keep track of what I want?

That's an excellent question, dear. As you can imagine, this is quite a challenge, the world being as big as it is. We have perfected a system that NASA would envy. Some of our Undercover Elves have in fact worked with the space program, borrowing some of the technology to streamline our Christmas mission. With so much information to stay on top of, we employ only the best and brightest List Elves to manage it. It all happens in Command Central, which is part of our Underground Annex.

Command Central

The heart of Command Central is the map room, which features a giant digital map that is linked to our special satellites. We can plot Santa's route in advance and make changes to avoid bad weather.

Next door houses the Master List. This is Santa's database of who's naughty or nice and what each child has requested for Christmas.

The Master List could not operate without the enormous mail room. Santa has a close working relationship with postal services worldwide. Undercover Elves, on special assignment as mail carriers, make sure your letters reach the North Pole without revealing its secret location.

Dear Mrs. Claus,

Where do Elves come from?

At one time, people and Elves had a lot in common. But as human societies became more civilized, complicated, and crowded, Elves moved underground, into the trunks of ancient trees, to the grottos behind waterfalls, and high onto misty mountaintops. They would come out only at night to play and, if not for their occasional mischief, were in danger of becoming forgotten. Luckily, Santa sent out a coded message using arctic fox couriers, inviting any Elves looking for a home and a job to join him here. Elves turned up in droves from all around the world.

Dear Mrs Claus,

How can I become an elf?

Well, for starters, no one can even apply who has not finished school. Only then can you begin Elf training. We look at our future Elves' records from an early age (remember we have one for everybody). Those who were kind to their siblings and schoolmates, helpful and obedient to their parents and teachers, and who took good care of their pets and toys, score high.

Elf Academy

As Santa's work became known throughout the world, letters began to arrive from kids and even some adults who wanted to become Santa's Elves. After a lot of thought, we decided that a select few would be allowed to join the new training school, the Elf Academy.

The program is long and difficult, but human Elves who complete it become our connection to the outside world. They are very helpful during the holidays when we make so many appearances to meet and greet our fans.

Many also work undercover in high-tech industries, toy companies, and postal services to keep us up to date. You can never be certain of who might be an Undercover Elf!

I know you've all wondered what the Elf Village is like. The buildings are all different styles depending on when they were built and which Elf tribes inhabit them. Some of the buildings look a lot like gingerbread houses and some have big rounded domes on top like igloos, and some even have turrets like castles.

Dear Mrs Claus, What do elves wear?

There is so much curiosity about the Elves since they are not seen in the human world. For practical reasons, all the Elves wear a similar uniform of warm leggings and a comfortable long-sleeved tunic or overalls. They are mainly in the same few shades of soft brown and moss green.

Elves love to accessorize. They are forever turning left-over scraps and bits from wardrobe and gift trimming into wonderfully colorful hats, scarves, jewelry, and adornments. These hand-crafted items are the gifts they typically exchange for Christmas, too.

The Elves each get two weeks of vacation a year plus two days off per week. Elves are hardworking souls but they live to have fun. They love sports of all kinds and are often playing outside or in the gymnasium. Quiet evenings are spent relaxing with board games, books, and jigsaw puzzles. Elves are always throwing parties, dances, and dinners, and inventing contests like cooking contests, talent contests, and even karaoke!

Dear Mrs. Claus,
What are the Elves' favorite books?

There are so many, it's difficult to list them all, but *Alice's Adventures in Wonderland, Charlotte's Web, A Wrinkle in Time,* and *The Wizard of Oz,* are all stories they never seem to tire of. Our magnificent library houses the complete collection of every fairy tale ever written (even a few you may not have heard of).

Dear Mrs. Claus,
What are their favorite songs?

It's safe to say pretty much all the Christmas carols, of course. Then there are quite a few favorites that are in the old Elfin languages, which I can't include here because the letters don't exist on my keyboard. Elves love to sing rounds too, but you won't catch Elves singing mushy love songs.

Of course all of you are familiar with Santa's famous eight. What you may not know is that the current team is only the latest generation of an ancient family of flying reindeer. Back in the olden days, many of the magical creatures, that have since become merely legend, really existed—unicorns, dragons, and talking cats. The air itself was different and lighter, and it was easier for animals to fly. The reindeer that lived far up in the Arctic became so good at flying that it became a kind of a specialty for them.

Dear Mrs. Claus,
Can all reindeer fly?

Certainly not. Modern reindeer have long ago lost the ability to fly, but here at the North Pole we have a breeding program to keep this rare genetic trait alive. Those reindeer that do not inherit the gene are assigned duties that assist us day to day. There is also a very special group who are not flyers, but possess exceptional speed, and are trained by Elf Jockeys for racing.

Dear Mrs. Claus,
How did the
reindeer get their names?

Some Elves knew where the last of the flying reindeer herds lived, so Santa sent special Scouts to bring back some young ones to train. The Elf Scouts who flew the reindeer back to the North Pole got to pick names they thought suited the reindeers' personalities. For the non-flyers, we have a contest to pick the name! Some of the names from contests past are Bristle, Piccolo, Arrow, Northstar, Linden, Brightly, Rufus, Tiptoe, and Verne.

Dear Mrs. Claus,
Are all the reindeer Boys?

Would it surprise you to learn they are not? Some of them are girls, though you wouldn't be able to tell by looking since they pretty much all look alike. Reindeer are the only type of deer where male and female both have antlers. We prefer it that way because we feel that all are equally special and wish to be treated the same.

Dear Mrs. Claus,
What do reindeer eat?

Oh that one gives me a chuckle, because I was about to say whatever they can get into! They seem to have a sweet tooth, just like the rest of the citizens up here. What we feed them though is a diet similar to what horses eat: mainly oats, sweet hay, and alfalfa.

Reindeer Stables

Our Flyers live in the original stables built not long after we first moved our headquarters to the North Pole. Since then we've built two additions to accommodate their children.

The west wing houses our Racers. Racing is a hugely popular sport here and both our Elf Jockeys and Racers are very competitive.

The east wing is where all the other reindeer live. These reindeer participate in regular work around the village: hauling supplies, moving toys from workshop to warehouse, and generally helping us get around. They love to join everyone for sleigh rides and sled races.

Dear Mrs. Claus,
How does Santa do it
all in one night?

Now that one's a little hard to explain. Between the hyper speeds the reindeer are capable of and the fact that Santa follows the path of the sun through the various time zones (plus a whole lot of magic), he always manages to empty his sleigh by sun up on Christmas Day. Everything is planned and rehearsed down to the tiniest detail—I see to that. Basically we begin to prepare for the following Christmas Eve on December 26!

Dear Mrs. Claus,
Who supervises everything
while all the work
is going on?

ow I don't wish to sound like I'm bragging, and I certainly couldn't pull it off without our team, but my main job is to make sure that everything runs smoothly. This is a fun job for me because the more there is to do, the happier I am. When I need to relax or take a little break, I bake a few batches of cookies or tend to my prized orchids in the greenhouse.

Dear Mrs. Claus,
How can Santa
get in if I don't have
a chimney?

Not to worry, dear. Santa doesn't need a chimney to visit. Now I probably shouldn't be telling you this, but we have perfected a tiny device, much like a wireless remote or garage door opener. It can bypass any alarm system and open any lock, and is small enough to fit on Santa's wrist! This is only one of our advanced tools and techniques, but the others must remain secret for now.

Dear Mrs Claus,
How does Santa fit all those toys in his sleigh?

It does take more than one trip to deliver all the toys. The garage is a combination launch pad and loading dock and it's where Santa's sleigh is loaded on Christmas Eve. Each time Santa returns to reload, an expert team of Elves quickly restocks the sleigh for the next run, while the Pit Crew de-ices the sleigh, waters the reindeer, and refills Santa's thermos. The reload can take less than ten minutes with all hands on deck!

Dear Mrs. Claus,
I saw Santa on T.V. and he didn't look the same!

This must be confusing, with all the many versions of Santa Claus and the North Pole on screen and on stage, but that's the price of popularity.

A person as famous and beloved as Santa is bound to be talked about, written about, and dare I say, even gossiped about.

But that's why I'm sharing all this with you now, so you know the real deal and can decide for yourself what to believe.

Dear Mrs. Claus,
I asked Santa for a...

bike

airplane

puppy

lizard

snake

dolphin

monkey

rhinoceros

dump truck

...and I didn't get one!

I know that many of you are wondering why, even though you were really good, Santa didn't deliver what you asked for. Santa carefully reads each of your special wishes. And sometimes no matter how much you would love your new pet or toy, Santa decides that it's not a good idea. But don't give up because if you wish, dream, or pray for something hard enough and long enough, you may get a happy surprise one day.

I'm afraid we've run out of time, but I've still got quite a few letters to answer. Perhaps we should wait till after Christmas for those. I've really enjoyed this little visit. But now I really must get back to work. It's our busiest time and there's so much to do. I really look forward to doing this again, so please send your new questions. I'll save them in my Top Priority File and let's set up another session sometime in the next year when things quiet down.

Have a very Merry Christmas! With love from Mrs. Claus

About the Author

Elsbeth Claus lives with her husband, Santa, and beloved cat, Miss Pippy, in a secret location somewhere north of the Arctic Circle. When she's not running their very well known international company, she enjoys yoga, baking, and gardening. She is especially proud of her rare orchids. This is her first book.

About the Illustrator

David T. Wenzel is an illustrator and children's book artist and has worked on many projects, including the Christmas bestseller *Rudolph the Red-Nosed Reindeer*, by Robert L. May. He is best known for his visualization of J.R.R. Tolkien's *The Hobbit*, illustrated in graphic novel format. David lives in Connecticut with his wife Janice. His studio overlooks a beautiful landscape of green farm fields and a winding brook.

Special thanks to Isabella, Mya, Faith, and all the children around the world for letting us publish their questions.

Copyright © 2008 by Christi Love
Cover and internal illustrations
© 2008 by David Wenzel
Cover and internal design
© 2008 by Sourcebooks, Inc.

Sourcebooks and the colophon are registered trademarks of Sourcebooks, Inc.

All rights reserved.

Published by Sourcebooks Jabberwocky, an imprint of Sourcebooks, Inc.
Naperville, IL

CIP data on file with the publisher